Chester Raccoon
AND THE
Big Bad Bully

By Audrey Penn
Illustrated by Barbara L. Gibson

Tanglewood • Terre Haute, IN

Published by Tanglewood Press, LLC, August 2008.

Text © Audrey Penn 2008.
Illustrations © Barbara Leonard Gibson 2008.

Design by Amy Alick Perich.

Tanglewood Press, LLC
P. O. Box 3009
Terre Haute, IN 47803
www.tanglewoodbooks.com

Printed in China

10 9 8 7 6 5 4 3 2 1

ISBN 978-1-933718-15-6

Library of Congress Cataloging-in-Publication Data applied for

*To Ellice, whose sweetness can
teach us all how to be better friends.*

hester Raccoon stood in front of his tree hollow looking gloomy. His younger brother Ronny and his best friend Cassy stood beside him.

"We don't want to go to school," Chester told his mother. "We want to stay home with you. Please. May we stay home with you?"

"I thought you liked school," said Mrs. Raccoon.
"We do," said Chester.
"Then why do you want to stay home with me?"

Chester lowered his head and shuffled his foot. "...er's...a... ully...a...ool," he explained in a quiet muffled voice.

Mrs. Raccoon reached out and tenderly lifted Chester's head with her hand. "What did you say?"

"Be brave," she told the cubs and gave each of her sons a comforting kiss in their palms.

After school, Chester, Ronny, and Cassy told Mrs. Raccoon how the badger bullied his classmates at recess.

"First he snatched a ball away from the squirrel and popped it.

"Then he climbed atop the jungle gym and squashed the opossum's fingers until the opossum fell to the ground.

"Then he spooked a doe, who bumped into the skunk, who got so scared that he sprayed and stunk. Even Owl Teacher couldn't get him to behave."

"Sometimes animals are bullies because they don't know any other way to be," explained Mrs. Raccoon. "But I think there's a way you can change things. Go get your friends and bring them to our tree. I want to share a story."

Boink!

Chester gazed into his mother's loving eyes and gulped. "There's a bully at school."

"And he's horrible!" cried Ronny. "He's big and mean."

"And he has giant claws on his hands and feet!" wailed Cassy.

"And fangs!" screeched Chester. "And fire comes out of his nose! And if you get in his way, he'll step on your face and squash you like a bug!"

"Like a bug!" echoed Ronny.

"Oh my! He sounds very scary," said Mrs. Raccoon. "Bullies can be very difficult! I'll tell you what," she told the frightened cubs. "I'll walk you to school and back. Then we can decide what to do about this bully."

When the raccoons reached the school tree, Chester tugged on his mother's arm. "That's him! That's the bully." He pointed a trembling finger at a badger standing by the pond. "Isn't he awful? Isn't he the most scary-looking bully you've ever seen?"

"Oh my, yes," whispered Mrs. Raccoon.
"But I'm sure we can work things out."
Before leaving, she gently fluffed Chester's
mask and playfully tweaked Ronny's nose.

A few minutes later, a crowd of eager young forest animals stood at the base of Chester's tree house, and Mrs. Raccoon began her tale.

"Once, a long time ago, there was a secret forest sprinkled in yellow stones. The stones were round and polished, big and little, and smooth enough to hold. Every animal in the forest collected and treasured them.

"One day, an animal found a blue stone! It was very exciting since no animal had ever seen a blue stone. But the blue stone was rough and dull, without any polish or shine. And it had sharp prickly points sticking out of it, making it very hard to hold.

"Careful not to hurt their paws, the animals carried the stone to the center of the forest and placed it atop a tree stump where everyone could see it.

"'Perhaps the stone is blue because it popped out of the ground too soon,' suggested a fox. So the animals waited and watched for many days and nights to see if the blue stone would turn yellow. But the stone remained blue, and its outer shell remained sharp and pointy.

"'I believe the stone is blue because that is the color it is meant to be,' said a very wise snake. 'Therefore, we shall treasure the blue stone for the color it is. But if we want to hold the stone, as we do our yellow stones, we'll have to work together to smooth its outer shell.'

"So first the woodpeckers took turns chipping off the stone's sharp prickly points with their beaks. Then the chipmunks rolled the stone with their noses, while other animals shined and buffed the stone with tree bark and fluffy tails. In time, the blue stone was as smooth and shiny as the yellow stones."

Mrs. Raccoon smiled down at the young animals listening to her story. "The badger at your school is just like that blue stone," she explained to Chester and his schoolmates. "He *is* a badger, and that is the way he is meant to be. But if you work together, I think you can smooth out his bullying ways."

The next day at school, when the recess bell rang,
all of the little animals went outside together.

School

They huddled close to one another and walked toward the bully in one great big confident pack, with Chester in front holding a ball.

At first the bully looked at them with a twinkle
in his eye, thinking, "I'll get one of you."

But as the pack got nearer and nearer to him without a hint of fear, the badger's expression changed. His eyes widened. His jaw dropped open. His knees grew weak and wobbly. Suddenly it was the bully who was scared.

He began to whimper and squeal and he thought, "They're coming to get me back." But there was nowhere to run. He just stood there, with his back up against a tree as his schoolmates drew closer and closer and closer.

Finally Chester was nose to nose with the trembling badger. He narrowed his eyes and looked as serious as his little furry face would allow. Then, without hesitation, he held up the ball, looked straight into the bully's eyes, and asked . . . "Want to play?"

"Huh?" The surprised bully stopped shaking. He looked at his classmates, who were laughing and offering friendship. "You want *me* to play with *you*?" he squealed with delight. He gently took the ball out of Chester's hands. "Okay," he told them. "I'll play." So in one short moment, the badger softened, and the bully became a friend. The badger didn't need to bully anyone ever again.

Chester glanced toward the wooded path and saw his mother
watching and smiling. She placed a kiss in her palm and showed it
to her son. Chester did the same and then joined in the fun.